I0536653

Timothée Roux

1

PROLOGUE

*And the Lord answered me and said. Write the
vision and make it plain upon tables; that he that
readeth it may run over it:
For as yet the vision is far off, and it shall
appear at the end and shall not lie: if it make
any delay wait for it: for it shall surely come,
and shall not be slack.
(Book of Habakkuk 2:2)*

ONE

When Louis heard Condoleezza Rice in March 2003 say "ignore Germany, forgive Russia, punish France", he took it personally.

Ignoring Germany was easy. He'd never go to a German restaurant, never learn this impossible language. He even took an oath never to take a summer vacation in one of their industrial cities.

Forgiving Russia. He believed in God. So he prayed. He prayed as his mother had taught him. He asked advice to his parish priest and together they prayed for Putin. That was a first, but he got over it. He forgave generously. He forgave what they'd done to political activists. He forgave what they did to their soviet comrades in Chechenia, Ukraine and elsewhere. Forgiving was purifying. It felt good not to hate Russians any more. Forgiving really brought the cold war to an end.

Then he set himself to punishing the French. Condi was clear. Times of landing on the Normandy beaches and dropping bombs were over. Punishing was essentially economic nowadays.

Louis knew how to do that. He could go a long way in punishing with his unique skill set. Economic punishment was definitely in his chords. And other types too... Ways that belonged to the 21st century, and to the next.

TWO

Bob Milkin was law enforcement. It seemed to him he could trace back his law enforcement lineage to the first policeman that ever set foot in the United States.

Every branch of his family was under a uniform of some kind. Mostly in the police. Some distant cousin here and there lost his way into the military. But men and women alike, they all served.

When Bob retired he couldn't completely hang up so he looked for things to do. He retired early in his fifties, victim of one of those budget battles, where Congressmen shut the purse on government that has no choice but to lay off. Nobody complains, because usually that means being hired back as a consultant with fifty percent more salary once the battle's over. So, he protected stars in Hollywood in the winter, joined some private patrols in Chicago in the summer. Even spent some months on oil platforms off the Nigerian coast to make up for the increasing tuition fees of his two kids. Training those Nigerian militias, shooting at high speed boats trying to storm his platform gave him more adrenaline than watching the Super Ball on his sofa with Nicole's friends.

What Bob missed during his whole career was something real big. He grew up dreaming of the times of Sam Houston when a state as big as Texas was on the verge of collapse and great men stood up to take it from the brink of disaster to one of the greatest states in the world.

Mass communication and later emails had killed initiative, and replaced it with careerism. His boss Tony used to laugh saying he knew old people, bold people, but had yet to meet an old and bold person. He knew he was gradually getting old and to the later stage of his career, and prayed he could prove Tony wrong.

Then Tony called him one morning.
- I'm in need of an old and bold monkey.
- I thought that didn't exist, Bob replied.
- Yes, I know. Joke aside, I've landed a big one, and I'd like you to take it.
- There's a team, Tony?
- No this time you're on your own. Can you drive up?

THREE

As Louis always said, if you do something, you might as well be the firstest to get the mostest. It's no use turning up once the lights are gone, or once the tickets are sold out. Everyone knows that the first in the queue on black Friday gets to choose. Louis never got there second.

He'd engraved on his door, "There is no substitute to Victory", and made sure to follow this quote from General MacArthur in everything he did.

Nature helped him a great deal. On the talent lottery, he got the top prize.
He outpaced the boys at school in every race.
He studied music instinctively.
He was bright, strong, and worked hard at anything that came his way.

Then his father bought him his first computer. He learned to code in all types of computer languages. Coding was his nirvana.

But the real fun began when he started cracking codes. That was better than Sudoku, better than Candy Crush or Clash of Clan. Better than cocaine. And free. Cracking firewalls was his new hide and seek, his new Olympics. He loved it and he excelled at it.

At school, Louis applied his newly acquired skills, and developed innovative ways of being first. He'd download the test from his

7

teacher's computer the night before, he'd get into the school's database to increase his marks a notch or two. But sometimes he just worked hard and outsmarted all the other kids. He was just gifted, and in an amazingly broad way.

He was the first to coin the phrase the "internet of things". He found out he could link things up like nobody could. Like no-one would think possible. For a long long time.

FOUR

Tony's office was a tribute to a long and successful career. A small museum to his ego, lined up with glass sculptures on the desk, unread books on the shelves, and walls lined up with caricatures of him young, or not so young. A large desk, created for times when paper was how you communicated, completely emptied nowadays, save a computer for reading emails and PowerPoints. Tony was part of that generation of leaders that didn't have paper any more, yet would never really learn how to use a computer. They lead with brains and guts. Data would wait.

- So what's up boss? Bob had never called him boss when he was working for him, but now that he'd moved on, he liked to pretend Tony was the boss. Maybe Tony still thought he was his boss. As a matter of fact, Tony always thought that hierarchy was never drawn on paper. Paper just tried to keep up.
- What is it that you know about drones?
- Well, I do have my own helicopter, which I like to fly over the house. You know Nicole's not fond of me flying it around the sofas and her pre-Columbian statues... So I fly outside but the wind is troubling me... I think I need a bigger engine.
Tony never interrupted anyone, which probably helped his career a bit, listening is a key skill for Hi-Po's, so Bob could have noodled on, but thought it wasn't fair complaining about Nicole, so he kind of paused, and looked up.
- I guess you didn't ask me to come because my neighbors are complaining about my helicopter flying above their swimming pool... The camera never worked by the way.

9

- Are the girls top-less? No sorry, I shouldn't make that kind of remarks. Might end up in the papers. Actually our neighbors *are* complaining.
- Tell me more.
- The French have shot down one of our drones that was flying over Paris last night.
- You guys are flying drones over Paris? You're kidding.
- Well the issue is, it's our drone, but we weren't flying it. We lost contact with this drone a week ago over the Panshir Mountains in Afghanistan. We thought it'd gone down.
- You've got an idea who's behind this?
- I may have a lead.
- And you've got the boys on it?
- I thought you may want to handle this one... Here's a picture of the drone, or what's left of it.
- Ok... A PBT-20 Gray Falcon?

Tony never acquiesced. This way you didn't know if he knew, cared, had moved on, or thought it gave him an air of superiority.
- It's hard to notice, but since we lost it, someone digitized a quote from General MacArthur inside the drone's command code, and I've got an idea who that could be.
- Family?

Tony did not answer. He walked over to his window, and slowly began nodding his head.
- When do I start?
- You've already started, still looking outside as if absorbed by the works going on in the opposite building. I called HR this morning. You're on.

10

FIVE

Go to the ant thou sluggard; consider her ways and be wise:
Which having no guide, overseer, or ruler,
Provideth her meat in the summer, and gathereth her food in the
harvest.
(Book of Proverbs 6:6)

Bob's idea of a geek fell apart when he got to Louis's. In his long career he'd met quite a few. Most of them perpetuated the stereotype of the first geeks, wearing long hair, pants knee high, smoking Marijuana, and working essentially at night listening to Heavy Metal. Even the folks two blocks down from his condo that'd repaired his broken laptop the year before belonged to this intellectual version of Bob Marley.

So when he came across a heavy built athlete that looked ready to pose for Boy Scouts of America's fundraising brochure, he asked for his way.
Louis on the other hand could spot police a long way off - at least the stereotyped versions Bob impersonated.

- Speeding ticket?
- I'm sorry. Bob thought he'd misheard. I'm looking for a gentleman, Louis...

11

- This an ID check?
- Umh... Not really. A... family visit.
Louis looked concerned all of a sudden.
- Is my uncle ok?
- Sure. Can I come in so we sit down for a chat?

Louis stepped aside waving his arm sideways like a policeman at a cross road, opening the way towards an Ikea furnished white washed condo. Not much furniture. A stool and a white melamine table in the middle of the room supporting a large computer without a recognizable brand on it. Climbing studs in the wall and ceiling, bars on the wall, and a strange looking bike in the corner with a computer screen and keyboard in front of it. With the shiny wooden floor and semi emptiness you felt like you'd stepped onto the bowling platform.

Louis produced a folding chair for Bob to sit on next to his computer.
- Do you need a drink?
- Coke?
- Sorry I've banned alcohol and soft drinks from my repertoire. I've got low sodium water from the Himalayas, ... sensational really.
- Sure, no ice...

Louis came back with two glasses and a tray.
- What's up? Tony sends you?
- Guess you know why...
- This is raking my brain. No. Why didn't he just call? Is it really family business? Doesn't look like a surprise birthday party from your I'll-put-you-in-a-cell look of yours.
- Drones?
- ...
- Now you know what I'm talking about.
- What is it that you know? I still don't understand why Tony's hiding.

12

- Your uncle doesn't meddle private and work affairs. You know that.
- His virginity.
- I beg your pardon?
- Nothing. So drones? You like drones?
- Did you fly a drone over Paris last week?
- Yes I did. Got some pretty cool pictures of Montmartre too. You want to give me up to Interpol? The French have issued a warrant?
- Not yet.
- Come on. Drones are everywhere, flying over the whole of France and elsewhere. Nothing wrong.
- You were flying a one million dollar military drone, Louis. Not a Walmart fifty dollar cracker.
- Ok, so that's the bad part. Are you FBI?
- I want to know how you got this drone.
- How do you know it's me by the way? I didn't admit. He jerked himself up a little to add some body bravado to his words, and Bob couldn't prevent himself from wondering what use such muscles were when you didn't belong to Special Forces. He noticed lately that men advertising body lotions also had strong torso so that may be who Louis was trying to emulate from. He got his mind back to Louis' fake denial.
- Well, you did admit. And you signed it on its tail. Not everyone likes to insert General MacArthur quotes in drone command codes these days. Louis, how did you get this drone?
- Well, I'm quite proud of it. Actually it's not that complex anymore. It's harder to steal sweets at the local bakery these days than it is to steal a drone. All you need is this, as he gestured towards his PC.
- This?
- Yep. You "just" need to get the IP address of the drone, overwrite the command software in the US Air Base, and there you go.
- Undetected?
- Completely. Just store your actions in the Tor network. This breaks apart your code into multiple elementary pieces that keep changing server around the world every minute. Like breadcrumbs

13

in a whirlwind. No-one can make up the shape of the bread anymore. That's pretty awesome actually.

- I still don't get it.

- What is it?

- How did you get a half fueled-up drone flying over Afghanistan five thousand miles west over to France?

- Aaah! That was awesome! I flew it over Ukraine, and got a Russian Tupolev to refuel. Ukraine sky is pretty congested these days with Russian aircrafts, so I just added to the confusion.

- You asked the Russians to refuel a US drone?

- Well, that was easier than a US refueler, right? They didn't ask as many questions. They just said we owed them one.

- Are you in the Air Base computer right now?

- I stepped out when the drone got shot. No use staying really. And you don't want to leave footprints all over the place by staying there for no reason. Not that the new contractors they use from Halliburton would notice the tiny footprints that I leave behind. But you never know. Another geek somewhere in Russia could recognize them and deep throat me to the KGB. Usually their allegiance is greater to the geek community than to the Soviets, but you never know, every once in a while, you get a nerd that doesn't respect the rules of the game.

- Well... you may have your own rules, but taking control of a US aircraft and flying it low over Paris isn't exactly following US rules. You're in trouble, Louis. Big time.

- O come on. I know why Uncle Tony didn't come down himself. It's not to separate private affairs from US interest. It's to avoid leaving a trace. So just leave by the back door, and tell Tony I owe him one. I'm sure this will be worth more one day to the US treasury than to put me behind bars. It will also avoid his sister digging her nails in his skull and wrecking his recent million dollar transplants.

Bob slowly rose from his seat, and made for the door. Dealing with family wasn't his thing. As he made for the door he paused and turned around.

- What was it that you were doing with a drone over Paris?

14

Louis chuckled.

- Ask Tony, this much he knows.

SIX

Bob's wake up routine was supernatural. For the last fifty years it had been rigorously the same. Listening to the BBC, or whatever scratchy noise he could identify as BBC World Service, and on his Nigerian rigs it was more a scratch than anywhere else. Then a series of press ups, although you couldn't tell from looking at his naked body. Then the same oatmeal, toast with homemade marmalade.

That morning of March 2014, the BBC was medium range scratchy in his DC condo, and the bulletin was full of the usual news. Bad news essentially, for even on the-stiff-the-upper-lip-world-service of Her Majesty's BBC, news is bad news. More blood in Irak, more deaths in Syria, kids abduction by Boko Haram, and a crash of a plane somewhere in Asia.

His phone rang.
He heard Nicole, who was in the bathroom.
- Do you pick it up, chéri?
Bob just moaned as he rose to get to the phone.
- Those commercial guys are real blood suckers. Vultures. They just go for your money. The phone bill seems only for them these days. And they don't understand no thank you, leave me alone. They're the modern Calcutta beggars of our time. They cling to your phone and don't let go. They don't want your politeness, they don't want form. They want money.

16

The phone kept ringing, so he grudgingly moved over. He lifted the receiver, not even bothering to say "Hi". That way the sound machine trying to sell him an insurance policy wouldn't even start.

- Bob, this is Tony.
He got the receiver closer to his ear.
- What time zone are you in?
- Same as you. Have you watched the news?
Tony's routine version of the BBC was Fox TV. GOP propaganda. Bob admired Tony for his astute sense of analysis but wondered if this wouldn't brain wash him over time.
- Kind of, I was shaving, so the journalist was speaking through foam and tap water.
- The Malaysian plane...
- The crash.
- I don't think it's a crash. They can't find a trace of it.
- What do you think it is? Crashes in the sea don't always leave traces...
- Why don't you come around? Once you've finished shaving of course.
There didn't seem to be much room for negotiation. The boss was concerned, Bob was back in the job.
- Thanks for the tip. See you then.

17

SEVEN

Tony hadn't told him much, once again. Bob was back on the United flight from Dulles to G. Bush Intercontinental. Taking off from Washington was something profoundly unique for Bob. Flying low over the main DC buildings and spearing up towards the sky gave him a sense of purpose. Some thrill deep inside. Like a rising of the flag on Independence Day. As the plane took off this time, he was thinking about the 9/11 hijackers who had tried to bring all of this down. He wondered what it had been to be inside that DC plane. His police brain tried to reconstruct the scene. Those terrorists must have jumped to the cockpit right after take-off to turn the Boeing on its wings and pancake into the Pentagon. They likely reached the clouds and veered back down... Maybe one of them was already in the cockpit at take-off. His mind switched back to his meeting with Tony, and wondered if the Malaysian flight too, had fallen under some Al Qaeda attack. He wasn't sure how Tony's nephew would play in this time. Would he find out things from this Einstein of the internet that no one would want to hear? He had got involved in his time in some big political drama, a case that pinned down the leader of the house with a pedophile gang. That was part of the job. Everyone was rushing to cover. Careerism was in great danger. Bob had stood on his own in the middle of the storm and cleaned it up. Ignoring threats, being drilled in Congress hearings, and working round the clock. So he was used to sh... hitting the fan. But this time he felt he was about to stumble on something beyond anything he'd seen so far. Tony's briefing didn't add up. He felt there were more things left out from the briefing than left in. Lawyers had turned the police jobs into a

18

big guessing game. Everyone needed to be able to say they hadn't been told. So the only guys that got the big jobs were those that understood without being told.

The plane was going through a series of potholes. This was hurricane season, so going to Texas wasn't nice. You never knew if you'd get stuck down there. He was starting to regret his gin and tonic. This Monday morning flight was unusually empty. It reminded him of flying into Bosnia in 1994. An Airbus 320 mostly empty, save a few diplomats, journalists, and some gun-happy war dogs. All heading to the Holiday Inn bar in Sarajevo, the only one Mladic hadn't shelled down.

As he got to Louis' apartment - a more expensive condo in the Heights than his former Rice Village loft, Bob had the feeling his discussion would be the same as the one he'd had a year ago. A visit for nothing. Fruitless and frustrating. Tony had never asked to be briefed in return. Bob had never gotten to the bottom of it. What had the two been up to? He'd never know. Bob never asked a question when he wasn't sure he'd get an answer. So he just didn't call Tony and Tony didn't call either. No debrief. It was surreal. A US military drone shot down over Paris and no follow-ups. Well, he assumed there had been some follow-ups. He'd just been left out of the loop. He was just a consultant. Everything on a need-to-know basis. Maybe this drone helped the French reduce one of their numerous D.o.J. fines.

As he rang Louis' doorbell he was expecting the same heavy built athlete from the Texan stud book. Instead an incredibly beautiful girl opened the door. As she opened her mouth to speak, Bob felt the same anguish he'd had as a teenager when talking to some awesome looking girl. Marriage hadn't changed anything.

- Can I help?
She must have repeated her question already, because she was looking at him with a smile that said she knew what effect she was having on him. And, she was damn used to it.

19

So when he settled in a comfortable sofa facing Louis, and she kissed Louis's forehead saying she'd run an errand, Bob was relieved. It was hard to imagine a meaningful discussion with Angelina Jolie's twin twitching her incredibly long legs in front of his eyes.

EIGHT

On the first floor of a noodle restaurant, in Hoi An, Vietnam, Miguel was happy.

Starting up a business in Vietnam wasn't easy, even in 2014. He'd tried starting up an IT business in Danang only to find folks wouldn't pay for that type of service. In communist culture, help was free. He'd set up the website of a new restaurant, only to be told that "sorry the manager didn't have enough to pay him, but thanks for the work". As a Spanish immigrant he wasn't supposed to start a company of his own anyway, so he couldn't go and complain to the police. He didn't even have a work visa.

So he'd gone to this new business of his. Working in Vietnam but operating out of Vietnam. As an IT service provider. For anyone, anywhere in the world. Sometimes simple ordinary stuff. More often than not, just small pieces of code. He wouldn't even know what the rest of the code would be like. But that was often the case in the IT world. Even during his internship at Gemini after graduating from the Scuela del Minas in Madrid, Miguel was coding stuff without knowing what the program was about. You had a start and a finish and you patched the middle piece. Like cutting cloth for a pocket without knowing if it would go on a pair of jeans, a coat, or as decoration on a wall.

So right now Miguel was happy. And it wasn't anything to do with the sweet and sour smell coming from the noodle shop below. Miguel's last piece of code had just been uploaded somewhere into cyberspace. It worked on diverting emitting radio signals and stopping any arriving signals. It had just been tested live and worked to perfection. He had got top markings in all ranking categories. That would likely trigger a move to a three star geek. His income would go up significantly, allowing him to pay the six thousand dollar annual tuition to the local Montessori school for his three-year-old Tina. She would learn English and get the best possible start in life. He didn't care for more.

What Miguel, and hundreds more like Miguel, did not know, was that they had just helped divert a major airliner off its route. The world of flight security was working round the clock on this lost plane, and no trace of it had been found. It's not that the missing aircraft hadn't mayday-ed or called for help. But the call never reached home, and the black box didn't even record the call.

Miguel deserved his third star. His work was near perfect.

NINE

Bob was used to others higher up the line making the big choices, and declaring victory. World War II had started with the invasion of Poland by the Nazi and Soviet forces, it had ended with the occupation of Poland by the Soviet. Yet this was big V victory - to be celebrated ever after. It didn't make any sense to him, but he knew it made sense for the guys dealing the chips. Nicole, who was big on Yoga, kept saying that giving in was the route to appeasement. Opposing yourself to the system lead to stress and frustration. "Practice not doing and everything will fall into place" was her favorite quote from this Asian bed side book of hers called the Tao Te Ching. So he would practice doing with Louis and not doing with Tony and everything would hopefully fall into place. Maybe.

- I've come to talk about the Malaysian airline.
- MAS 370, KL to Beijing, 227 passengers and 12 crew members missing, Louis replied as if he was participating in a TV quiz.
- Merde.
- I'm sorry?
- Did you divert it like the drone?
- Sure not. I'm not insane. How would I feed 239 people, babies and all? No, fuck no.
- What happened?
- You're asking me? Well, something happened. Storm, failure, explosion, who knows?
- Electronic take-over?

23

- Possible.
- Is there a way of checking?
- Well, there is. But I'm not sure you care knowing about it.
- Tell me.
- No matter where this leads you?
- No matter.
- You answered too quickly.
- No... matter.. where...this...leads...me.
- Ok, dickhead. It's a long story.
- I've got all my time.
- Have you ever heard of Wiki-Terror?

TEN

Stefan Brokevic was born in Belgrade in 1969. He changed his name to Slobo on May 8, 1989, the day Slobodan Milosevic, ex Wall Street lawyer was elected president of Serbia. Stefan's dad taught law at University and quickly spotted the young Milosevic. For all their flaws, communist countries were all on identifying talent early. So, with the rest of the Intelligentsia, Stefan's dad made sure the talented Milosevic got the best training to fill the vacuum Tito would eventually leave at his death in 1980. Slobodan graduated from law school, got one of those apparatchik training jobs at the national oil and gas company, then moved quickly to the top job at Beogradska Banka, the leading bank of the country. So when six months before the fall of the Berlin Wall, Stefan graduated from IT engineering school and Milosevic became the first president of the Republic of Serbia, the Brokevic family celebrated with much vodka and by changing Stefan's name to Slobo.

When men get to power, the first thing they need are men of complete trust. Young Slobo met these criteria and his IT skills would come in handy when managing Milosevic's personal secretariat. He followed the newly elected president everywhere, organized Milosevic's appointments, and gradually became the man to know in the president's entourage to get access to the great man. Things got pretty rough quickly. In 1992 Yugoslavia blew apart, and everyone went crazy both inside and outside the country. Every Yugoslav had his weapon. In the past that had enabled them to be the only European country to free itself from the Nazis without extra help. Now they were turning the same weapons against one another. Creating some of the worst bloodsheds of the 20th century. The bar had been set pretty high by Mr. Hitler and Stalin, but they got pretty close. And no-one seemed to care. Peaceful Europe went ablaze and discovered itself still capable of the worst atrocities. Eventually the Clinton administration got sick of it all, and sent in Richard Holbrook plus a few guided missiles. Richard's high flying temper found its match with Milosevic's and both of them started drawing the lines of post war ex-Yugoslavia, in what was to become known as the Dayton peace agreements. Behind the scenes wasn't always clean, but peace has its own cost. Both leaders had their go-to men to organize everything around them, from safety, to drafting pre-reads, to back stage agreements. Slobo on one side, a certain Bob Milkin on the other side. Holbrook wanted police specialists that had worked abroad and open to the cultural diversity of the Balkans. Bob was his top pick.

Bob was twice Slobo's age, but both meant business, and both wanted peace. They learned to respect one another for their unique efficiency. They got things done. A rare skill that those who possess recognize immediately in others.

That they could secure peace almost overnight surprised the whole world. When in a Northern US air base, chosen for its remoteness, the Dayton agreement was signed, both men returned to their normal jobs. Both had the sense of accomplishment. History may not remember them. But they would never forget what history owed them.

Unknown to Bob, Slobo also left with a permanent ID access to the Pentagon intranet. He would watch Bob because he sensed anything big would go his way, so it was the most efficient way of watching Uncle Sam.

When the US started bombing Belgrade a few years later, completely amnesic that they were bombing an ally, Slobo started

26

looking for revenge. And Bob looked like a good place to start. In the old mafia tradition he would start with a threat with no harm. Almost a gift. A box of hand grenades. And gradually move up the scale. His IT skills would find a path that Bob would never be able to trace back to him.

ELEVEN

The Heights is one of the most sought after places in Houston. By both the wealthy and mosquitoes. Fort Bend County had declared war on the bloodsuckers and had started spraying chemicals. But like the Vietminh, those mosquitoes were clearly meaner and tougher than the chemicals that were being spread. This year mosquitoes were even carrying West Nile Virus. Bob expected Louis to be ill equipped so he had sprayed from ankle to ear with the same repellent he'd taken in Nigeria. He smelled of toilet deodorant and his skin was itching but he felt safe.

The light was fading on Louis' balcony and Louis had just gone back to light two scented candles. The oriental fragrance reminded him of Nicole. Maybe she bought the same candles.

What Louis had just told him was gigantic. So monstrously big that he wondered how much was true. What if the guy was just a maniac story teller? A nerd who'd stayed some hours too many in front of a computer screen. Another Russel Crowe in "A Beautiful Mind". Maybe Louis' story was only true in this parallel world of his where he was imagining things.

Issue was MAS 370 had disappeared and Mr. Muscle Louis had an explanation. Wiki Terror.

According to Louis it all started long ago.

28

- You see, there was Wikipedia for knowledge. An encyclopedia. Well, you could tell lies, truth, and propaganda. Usual stuff. Not much different than Encyclopedia Britannica.

Ok, so Wikipedia, then WikiLeaks, and a few other Wikis. But nothing real. "Am Anfang war der Tat".

- Goethe, Bob replied who'd studied German because spying on East Germany was where most spying careers started in the old days.

- So I thought if we could all do something small, we'd be able to achieve something big. So the thought grew in my head, and eventually I started coding. I tested my code and it worked.

- With a drone?

Louis chuckled.

- Wow. No. With a grain of rice.

- You diverted a grain of rice.

- Absolutely.

- Ethiopia was dying. So I did a human chain from Nepal to Ethiopia

- With a grain of rice

- You got it.

- And that worked.

- Sure. The key was to get the grain in more than ten thousand hands. And for no one to know what he was really doing.

- You were the only one.

- Yes. And when the grain of rice arrived, no one knew it had happened. Think of this grain of rice as a spy. Sent to watch on all the other grains of rice. Could have gone back to Nepal to tell his pals.

- Amazing.

- Then I set up a system that made people decide what to do. A kind of ranking system. If everyone wanted to send rice to Ethiopia, then rice would shuttle. If people didn't want it to flow to Ethiopia, it would stay in Nepal or go to Walmart.

- So what happened?

- Well you saw the news. Ethiopians just continued to die. People were ok with them dying. Democracy. Like it or not.

29

- But all your work for nothing.
- Bullshit no. This was Wiki-action. This was big. Real big.
- Wiki Action. No Terror.
- Not yet. Not... just yet.
- So tell me what happened.
- Well, I'd been playing and tuning my system around a bit.
Got thousands of adopters, tens of thousands, then millions. Got coders too. Coders I'd never met. Open source. And it worked, things started happening. That was democracy on a world scale. The masses wanted something, spelt out, ranked it high, then ten thousand invisible hands would comply not knowing what they were doing. Fully transparent. Man, I was watching democracy in action.
- Then what.
- Then the US invaded Irak. Despite a big bunch of hypocrites, despite old Europe. Despite WMDs, despite Saddam, despite being shown on TV. Only the US could figure out what to do. Then Condi said out loud what you could already feel on the web. Wiki Action was rumbling. Condi just tipped the scales.
- What do you mean?
- "Ignore Germany, forgive Russia, punish France". Remember her quote?
- ... What the hell ... did you do?
- I plugged her quote into Wiki Action. Gave it the highest ranking. I can influence the ranking a bit. And soon afterwards, Wiki Action became known in the IT community as Wiki Terror. By a few aficionados at first who saw it coming.
French CEOs starting falling like stricken flies. Jean-Luc Lagardere in 2003, Edouard Michelin in 2006. Almost every single French company in the last eleven years has lost his highest ranking official and got massive D.o.J. fines.
- And the CEO's of the two energy companies, Total and Areva, in 2014?
Louis nodded.
- There's no timing protocol on the internet, so you don't always know when things will happen. They just happen. With ten

30

thousand individuals that committed the crime without knowing and millions that voted for the crime yet didn't do it, there's simply nothing that the judiciary can do about it. This is democracy. Big D.

- You could be charged for the crime. Sorry the crimes.
- I didn't commit any crime. I just coded.
- A code that killed.
- It's open source. Anyone can read the code and modify it. You just need to outvote the crowd and that's impossible. It's natural. It's like a volcano or a tsunami. They kill yet don't go to jail. Crime is for individuals. A crowd doesn't commit crimes.
- So how does it all end? When you don't have a French CEO left standing. Is this it?
- Or when the crowd gets tired. And moves off to something else.

Bob was just pondering where to go with that story. What to make of it. What could be done to stop it. He couldn't see the link with the Malaysian Airline plane.

- Is MAS 370 being diverted or shot down by Wiki Terror?
- Well, partially, but this discussion is really going to take a while.
His girl had come back and said:
- You want to sleep on the couch? It's past midnight.
Bob's phone rang.
- Hey Nicole, what's up?
- Are you at your hotel? Who's this girl I'm hearing in the background.
- I'm still interviewing.
- Who's she?
Bob could feel the voice getting a bit dry at the other end. He wanted to answer, "it's my tennis teacher", but thought it wouldn't be wise.
- I'm still at work. I can't talk right now.
Nicole hung up. Bob was staring at the back page of a Wall Street Journal on the table in front of him, where an IBM ad said "a smarter decision made by millions of Tweets. There's a new way to

31

decide". Bob felt the whole world was conspiring. A gigantic conspiracy. Did anyone know? Everyone except himself? Maybe he was getting like the guy in "A Beautiful Mind".

While Bob was on the phone, Louis had walked over to the kitchen and had returned with another pitcher of some strange looking liquid. Almost fluorescent.
- Want a glass?
- Will that make me glow in the dark?
- Even better. Gooseflesh all over.
- Sure.
- You want to see on my screen how it works? Or you want to know more of it? I can teach you how to divert a school bus, a car, or a plane if you like. It's fun. You don't have a CCTV inside the vehicle you're disrupting, but you can imagine the surprise you're creating. I think the first planes they used Wiki Terror on, were the 9/11 planes.
- You're kidding me.
- You really think that ten hours of mono engine plane rides in Minnesota will teach you how to glide a Boeing into the middle of the Pentagon? Come on, you know better than that. You needed those guys to wave their cutters at the crew so that they'd bugger off. You needed the world to think that this was hijacking. But you needed Wiki Terror to make it work. Even the streets of Cairo know that Al Qaeda is not capable of organizing such an attack.
- But you said you needed scoring.
- Well America's not loved much these days. So yeah, unfortunately this got a pretty high score, and the volunteers' chain started building up. Of course the hijackers thought they were hijacking. They actually sat in the cockpit. But my god, they would have crashed the plane somewhere stupid. Not in the middle of the towers. No way.
The Toyota recalls were all Wiki Terror's too. Hatred of Japanese hurting Detroit and our gas eating pick-up trucks.
But this Malaysian plane troubles me, because I think there wasn't anyone in the cockpit. So that would mean the code's made some

significant progress again. I need to find out how they did this. I need to dig into this. That's the magic of open source and why nothing in the world can beat it. I'm on my own, so I cannot watch what thousands of coders are developing as we speak. I can catch up pretty well though. I'm still probably one of the best at the game. But man, you need to stay on your toes, because those kids out there are real smart.

- Can you look it up while I sleep on that couch, and tell me in the morning?

- You need to put me under arrest, otherwise, I'm going to sleep with Cinderella tonight.

- Well you're pretty much under arrest. It's just a question of doing the paperwork. And Cinderella is too, so you'll stay together. We have dual careers now in the police.

As Bob got to the couch, he checked out his emails. Tony had insisted on him taking a Department iPad and not using his personal laptop for this piece of work. Congress was getting all hooked up on Hilary having used her private account as State Secretary, so the whole US administration had to adhere to new guidelines. Quite a waste actually. As a consultant he didn't get many emails anyway. Just a couple of emails, the first being a safety training reminder, that bore the ominous Nobody Gets Hurt wish in the title. He didn't quite understand where the department was heading. Nobody Gets Hurt seemed ok in a school, but how did you apply that in the Police. He was glad to be on the other side for now. He'd probably get some angry reminders for not having taken his online safety course. An excited training manager would yell at him for not doing more actively caring. Maybe Tony would get a call from HR. His second email was titled "Mock Phishing Attack Notification". Content of the text said "Cyber security threats continue to rise, with data breaches at major corporations and government departments lately". It concluded by saying that "the most efficient defense is awareness". The orchestra kept playing as the Titanic went down, Bob thought.

33

He woke up a couple of times. Having told Louis not to sleep meant he kept typing at his computer, and his lady Godzilla kept coming back wrapping her long body around him, in more and more alluring attire as the night dragged on. Their lovers' whispers became part of his dreams. This mission was definitely not going right.

TWELVE

Nicole loved her tennis lessons. She had been in the college team back in France, her native home land. She played juniors at Roland Garros, and had made it to WTA100 when she met Bob. Her moving to DC, then around the world as the hunt on terrorists went global, and raising Jeff and Bob junior wasn't the best way to move to the next stage of a tennis career.

Mentally though, she hadn't given up. That was part of her DNA. She took tennis like some take cocaine. Her goal was to beat ex grand slam winners on the senior track. With less experience but less body wear, and with her game as it stood, she stood a good chance of fulfilling her dream.

This Tuesday morning, she was off with her coach to practice on grass ahead of a UK tournament. The change of surface was always difficult on her, but she liked the challenge, and didn't want to put all the eggs in one basket by focusing her game on one surface only.

Her coach Luigi was known to have coached some of the best athletes of his time. His perfect sun tan and V shape body made Bob a little nervous. Nicole kept telling her husband that Luigi had much younger and better flesh to lay on than hers, but he wasn't sure she understood everything about male appetite.

Luigi was already there when she arrived. After completing a few laps to warm up, she took off her Nike jacket and went to take a few balls from her box. As she opened, she started.

- Come on lazy ass! Luigi called, the grass is waiting.
She closed the lid slowly.
- Hey! Wake up! We need some balls!
- We'll take yours this time if you don't mind.

She jogged back to center court. Just before that, taking a snap shot with her iPhone of her tennis balls and sending it to Bob, with just a short text "do you know why my tennis balls have been replaced by small plastic bombs?" Maybe he'd regret not having slept with her last night after all. Years back in Paris, a young American whose company she was starting to appreciate had offered one evening to become her bodyguard, till death us part, he had added. She had laughed, but when he repeated his offer a month later, she had simply answered "sure". What she hadn't realized was that Bob meant it, and he would make thorough checks every evening, even checking his German pistol in his bedside table.

Had he been there the night before, he probably would have noticed that her tennis ball box had been touched. She was almost certain.

But so did the folks that removed her tennis balls, and replaced them with plastic hand grenades.

THIRTEEN

Bob woke up drowsily. He hadn't taken a shower the night before, had slept all dressed up, and now his Nigerian anti-mosquito cream was starting to peel off. Or maybe his skin too. He should have checked the expiration date before spreading it thick all over. He glanced at his phone. It said 7am Houston time. Nicole must be on her tennis court. She'd even left him a text. Which got him straight up in a second.

- That text got you up all right, sheriff.
- We need to talk. Read this, as he handed his iPhone over to Louis.
- What's up? You're sure this isn't classified material? Louis said, pretending to refuse to take the phone, but taking it reluctantly. But yep, sure we need to talk, I found a few things while you were snoring off the couch, Pa.
- What do you make of it?
- Well, before playing Daniel with your dreams, why don't I tell you what I found? That may explain your text.
- Tell me about my text first.
- You have a WikiTi profile.
- A what?
- Remember anything from last night?
- ... yes.
- Well you have a WikiTi, a Wiki Terror profile.
- Why me?
- Well that's what most people have. Your wife has one. Your kids have one. If you have a Facebook, a Twitter account, almost any

37

kind of internet existence, then you end up with a Wiki Terror profile.

- Nicole has one.

- Sure. But hers is pretty quiet right now.

- So this is for me.

- Well your negative scoring right now is pretty low, so that's the only thing you can get right now. I wouldn't worry more than if a guy driving a pick-up truck did you a middle finger. Sure people love you, others hate you, that's freedom of speech, nothing wrong with that.

- You mean people threaten me with plastic grenades, and there's nothing wrong.

- It's not the mafia you know. This isn't like the God Father. Brando isn't after you. They didn't send you the head of a horse as a warning that they were going to kill you. It's democracy, relax. Calm down.

- I don't relax. You did this.

- The world did this to you, pal. Wake up, this is the 21st century. The crowd, the cloud.

- They shouldn't put a retired man on such a job. I can barely click the mouse.

- Well you've got me, grand pa. I think you need a coffee.

- Thought you only had Himalayan water.

- Well most of the time. Sometimes, Himalayan mud gets in the mix, say try this.

- Urgh.

- You want to hear about this Malaysian airline, Sir?

- Press on.

- Ok, so I think this is the first airplane in history that's been hijacked without any hijackers.

- What is this supposed to mean?

- Well, you have tens of thousands of hijackers that scored against the plane passengers, but nobody was on the plan to highjack it. Does that make sense?

- So where is it?

38

- I think it's landed somewhere, but it's hard to see. I told you I coded Wiki Terror so that any data and piece of the code would change server every minute inside the Tor network without leaving any trace.

- Yes, I remember, bread crumbs in a whirlwind.

- Right, you must be a visual kind of man. So I find some echo here and there that says the plane landed but I don't know where. And the Japs and US navy left land strips on almost every single island in the South Pacific so the guys could have pancaked almost anywhere. They could be on a paradisiac island or eaten by some of the last remaining man eating tribes in Indonesia. A pretty cool kind of mystery for a policeman, I'd assume. We try not to have torture or death penalty in WikiTi. Folks just get lost. A bit like re-incarnation. Half of the geeks worldwide are from India, so what would you expect?

- So how many more planes your Wiki thing is going to turn around?

- I guess more and more. It's open source and the code is progressing fast. They're a few days I think from being able to highjack simultaneously a large amount of cars. Steering, speed and all. They could send I10 at rush hour in the ditch like mad animals rushing off a cliff. Or keep folks driving on Beltway 8 round and round until they ran out of fuel, without being able to get out. Wait till we get the un-manned car. This will get real fun. I hope we don't scare them before they mass produce it.

- Bob, can't you keep the scores down?

- That's not in the spirit of the code.

- Fuck the spirit. This is fucking Armageddon!

Louis starting pacing the room like a stricken tiger. A mad boxer looking to strike. The night spent working on his screen had made his eyes red, giving to his sudden anger a dangerous look of madness.

- This is democracy grand pa. It's no use having been hypocrites all your life up there in your beloved Capitol Hill. This is true democracy. Sometimes it will be ugly, but my guess it will be less ugly than Vietnam, or Hiroshima. It will regulate itself. Let it go.

39

The communists tried to regulate the market and failed miserably. If you try to regulate Wiki Terror everyone will want to regulate it, think of it. I won't un-code my jewel, not if you forced me to. This is my baby! I think you've learned enough to go and make a report in your elegant hand writing to emperor Tony of DC.

Have a great day, and don't try to water board me, or your score will go overboard instantaneously!

FOURTEEN

Bob had gone straight from Dulles airport to the office. Putting calming Nicole and his now reddish peeled-off skin behind what he viewed as his duty. Time was of the essence he thought, and unlike the terrified SS who dared not wake up the Fuhrer on June 6 1944 to tell him of the Normandy landing less his anger would send them to concentration camps, Bob didn't care if his looks ruffled Tony. Saving the world came first.

With hindsight, it may have helped his case to come in cool as a cucumber and smelling of the latest Eau de Cologne from Hermes Nicole had brought him back from her last trip to visit her ailing mother in Paris.

- So you've joined the band of conspirationists Bob. You of all men! Who would have thought my cool brained hero would one day turn up dressed like a ruffian, telling me repent the end is near, Armageddon is coming. This is the end.
- Funny ha-ha.
- Bob, the twin towers fell because of two planes hijacked by Saudi terrorists who had been promised one hundred virgins each, and because our friends across the street at CIA didn't read the reports that landed on their desks. Even the head of the IMF is ready to lose everything for a dozen virgins, Bob. So, when you think of it...
- Tony, if you sent me there, it's because you were interested in what I'd found...

41

Tony started fumbling with his pen, and Bob didn't know what perky joke his former boss was preparing. Sometimes witty remarks were obsessive with Tony. Getting the upper hand rhetorically captured his entire competitive mind. So of all the potential answers he didn't expect the one that followed.

- You're in Bob.
- What's that supposed to mean?
- You take our entire IT department, you've got full powers across all government departments until we've got the solution to this new IT war. We're at war Bob. And the enemy, like the mythological Hydra, has a thousand heads.
- Tony, I'm a consultant. I can help. Not much more than that. I'm retired.
- Bob, that's an order. From the President.
- Why me?
- We don't hire men like you anymore, Bob. Even before the millennials came in, folks were caring sixty percent for themselves, forty percent for the department. I can't win a war with part timers.
You'll be all right. I just need you to lead our IT efforts for a while.
- Thanks.
- You'll find them waiting for you. By the way IT is on the third floor these days, you can't miss them.

SECOND PROLOGUE

Writing a novel is as if you are going off on a journey across a valley. The valley is full of mist, but you can see the top of a tree here and the top of another tree over there. And with any luck you can see the other side of the valley. But you cannot see down into the mist. Nevertheless, you head for the first tree. At this stage of the book, I know a little about how I want to start. I know of the things that I want to do on the way. I think I know how I want it to end. This is enough.
(Terry Pratchett, 2000)

FIFTEEN

March 8 2014 - Roger just got out of a meeting with the Malaysian oil company Petronas' top brass. Li Peng Xui, self-baptized Roger when he graduated from Shanghai University, belongs to China's cream of the cream. Identified at the age of eight as particularly gifted by Deng Xiaoping's talent detectors, Roger was hereafter separated from his family and sent to the best teachers of the Communist Republic of China. After Shanghai University he went to do a PhD in oil seismics at Berkeley, where he broke all records. Highest number of patents, highest number of publications, and key breakthroughs. It goes without saying that every oil company in town was desperate to have him sign a contract. But unlike many of his fellow citizens lured by a better life in the US, Roger was programmed to go home, and help China become the world's leading superpower.

Now in his late forties, Roger leads the oil M&A Strategic Department of PetroChina. He made PetroChina value overtake all others including Apple and ExxonMobil, but he intends to go much further. As Malaysia readies itself for its Grand Prix that will take place in less than three weeks, Roger readies himself for a much bigger deal that will crown his already fantastic career. Something that will consecrate the hegemony of China in the West Pacific and secure its energy independence once and for all. Roger knows China cannot beat the US without its own oil.

Roger has spent the day on the Sepang circuit, rushing adrenaline with his business counterparts at the wheel of a Porsche GT3. As

44

he steps down, the brake pads are literally on fire. So is his joy. When President Li comes over in three weeks for the Grand Prix's most important meeting, he will probably share the same kind of feeling.

Gifts are exchanged and left untouched following the Asian tradition, before everybody parts. When it's time to go, Roger looks at his watch. It's past eleven o'clock. This dinner took less time than usual, despite the everlasting toasting with Sake. If he's quick he can rush to the neighboring KL airport, and get on today's last flight to Beijing. That would get him around 8am at the office the next morning, allowing him to have a full day of efficient work. He's going to make a dash at it. He jumps in his awaiting limo. Road is quick at this time, yet the police escort pretend the make themselves indispensable with their wailing sirens. They wave aside the odd cattle cart one still finds on motorways in that part of the world, almost standing on their motorbikes. Roger is driven straight to the foot of the plane, and a glance at his watch tells him as he sits down it's just 12:30, He reclines his seat as the engines of MAS 370 are brought into action. A day well spent, without a minute lost. China's future cannot wait.

Despite the flight attendant gesturing at him to shut down his device, he manages to send his wife a quick text "Darling I've been lucky, I finally managed to get on tonight's flight". A text she'd never forget and that would haunt her nights for a very long time.

SIXTEEN

Bob had seen so many retired officers continue to wear uniform like veterans from the First World War, long after both their body and their mind had started their long march downhill, that he had made a vow never to wear his uniform after retirement. So when he came in the day after his interview with Tony, he wore what he thought should be the uniform of a police department consultant no matter how senior. Grey flannel trousers, a white long-sleeved shirt, and a black jacket and a tie. Nicole told him that made him looked like a priest. "Are you contemplating a second career as a clergyman?" she told him pretending to unbutton his shirt as he was getting ready to climb into his Chevy.

Chief inspector Fiona Prescott welcomed him her mouth twitching into a sneer. She wasn't delighted to have some unknown civilian suddenly take charge of the department. This wasn't going to be easy. Bob wasn't sure what Tony had told her. Probably had avoided a fight by not defining too clearly Bob's role, and supervisor relationship he would have with her. She would probably try to sink him while trying to pretend she was helping. Knocking you out by throwing the life buoy on your head. Some got so much practice throughout their career...

- How would you like to start?
- Fiona, why don't you gather everyone.
- What do you mean everyone? We can meet here with my three direct reports if you wish for a group meeting. Let me call them.

46

- I'd rather have everyone. The whole department. Clerks, operationals, everyone.
- That's rather unusual. Not sure people will understand what is going on. Let's first align with the department heads.
- Fiona, what I need to say is of critical importance. And I don't want it deformed and delayed down the chain. It's 7:50, can you get everyone out from their offices for 8:00?
- Sure, anything is possible, we can ring the fire alarm and get everyone on the front lawn for you.
- Whatever suits you, but I'd rather do it indoors if that's ok for you.
This wasn't going to be easy. Job transitions were always difficult and you had to kowtow to everyone first. And the best transitions were those where your predecessor vanished and kept out of the limelight. This time, she was right there, still vaguely in charge, and he had no time to waste. This wasn't going to be easy. As everyone started gathering outside their offices and cubicles, you could hear the noise level going up.
- Ahem.
Getting them to shut up was going to be his first challenge.
Fiona took pity of him, or maybe that was just to make him look awkward. She shouted at the top of her lungs.
- Silence fore and aft!
Goodness, Bob thought, some ancestor in the Royal Navy, or what?
- Ladies and gentlemen, I have something important to say. While you've been focusing on pedophile gangs on the net, North Korean cyberattack on Sony, and Russian geeks hacking into the State Department intranet, something much bigger has been going on unnoticed.
He paused to create some kind of suspense. Some were just sneering at him, others started giggling, others looked sleepy, and some started looking at their smartphone. That's my army, Bob thought.
- Open source terrorism.

47

He paused again trying to sound convincing, but barely convincing himself. Three of them, all men, at the front, probably her three lieutenants, were shaking their heads in disbelief.

- I want you to hunt down open source terrorism. Something that can highjack your car, your plane, your refrigerator.

He didn't know why he added that because it got them all laughing as if he was the alternative humorist at their annual Christmas Party.

- We strongly suspect the Malaysian airline flight to have gone down from open source terrorism.

A few lifted their heads. He had the impression some already started walking back to their offices. Fiona next to him took his elbow, and said.

- I think we should get back into my office.

- Do you have any questions? Bob threw out to the audience, elbowing himself out of Fiona's grasp.

- Who's we? Why don't those that suspect those Malaysians track them down? Are we supposed to let the pedophiles lose, and sing Kumbaya with the Russians and Koreans? None of this makes any sense.

The very large guy in front of the crowd, was probably one of Fiona's department head, playing ball with her. A rambling noise of lose discussions started, and he thought he heard someone at the back say:

- Who the heck is he?

I'm not starting a Question and Answers session here, Bob thought, so he added on.

- For the next five days, I want every one of you to focus on finding anything on the web that looks like a cyberspace hijacking signal. I want you to look for any vague signal from one of the passenger phones. Folks out there are searching the sea. I want you to search the cloud. Look for three to five lines of code at a time. Look at the Tor network. Don't expect this is going to be easy. And I want you to work round the clock. We'll be bringing in meals and mattresses in. Call your families. You're stuck for the next five days. Now get going.

48

If that was supposed to jerk them into action, that seemed to fail miserably. Maybe he underestimated the power of the uniform. The only flannel suited men those guys saw these-days, were white collars caught watching child porn on the internet. He daren't even look up at Fiona, not wishing to know if she was wearing that look of condescending victory. Another sneer in her seemingly infinite catalogue of grimaces.

Bob turned around feeling somehow miserable, and got back to Fiona's office. She opened fire as soon as the door closed on them.

- So what exactly do you want them to do? Maybe we can reboot this whole process? Why don't you tell me what you're after? We need a process, we need tools, we need methods. This is the US IT police department. Not a family gathering. You don't send men to the moon by shouting "get up there folks, you have one week to land a man on the bloody moon". That's the f..king look you saw in their faces. They don't mind helping. But they need your help too! There's a power structure, Mr. I don't know your name. If you don't go through me, you won't achieve anything! And I won't help you.

One of the three guys from the front row, stepped in.

- Mind if I join the debrief? I'm Tamid.

- What do you suggest we do, Tamid, Fiona asked him.

- This gentlemen needs to give us his facts, his indices, and from there on we'll look if there is anything we can do for him. I'm not at all sure we can help anyways. We get conspiracy theories ten times a day. From folks with high connections. We've got shit loads of crazy guys thinking the end is near with connection to Capitol Hill, who land on our door step to revolutionize this department. They'd rather we looked elsewhere than in their dirty little tricks, most of the time. Fathers of state secretaries or even presidents step in telling us how we should run things. We're never short of advice.

- Why don't you start telling us what it is that you know, and then we'll see if we work on it? Fiona said. Bob thought, so much for Tony asking him to lead the IT teams for a while. Tony's way of never saying no to anyone, of pleasing everybody, everywhere, all the time.

49

- Ok, Bob said, so here is the story. We have evidence that the internet is moving away from its traditional model of collecting data and sharing it, to something more actionable, that can derail trains, change the route of a commercial airline. I want your guys to screen the internet, including the Tor network for anything that looks connected to this Malaysian airline. There's not more to it.

- Ok Tamid said, I'm going to put someone on that immediately.

- I want everyone, Tamid, not just one person.

- I'll put my best one, it will be better than everyone. Some of them can't even type. Leave this to me, I know how to run this shop. Judge me on the results.

Another guy poked his head around the door.

- Are we only interested in the internet?

- Yes, Bob answered.

- Art, you're not working on this, you're tracking the Cincinnati Gang. Fiona cut in.

- Well, if I'm not supposed to track the Malaysian airline, and you don't want me on the case, I'll keep what I found for myself.

- Cut that crap, dickhead, Fiona interrupted with her usual gutter slang. Not the first woman in a man's world thinking vulgarity was necessary to cut her way up, Bob thought.

- Ok, Malaysian police assume the plane to have crashed forty one minutes after take-off, which is when they lost contact with the aircraft. As you said "look on the internet", I thought I'd look elsewhere. Does that make sense? He giggled not bothered nobody else was sharing the joke.

Art continued.

- So this is what your cute face little Art did. He looked at satellites. This gentlemen said look at the cloud, or the sky, I don't remember which. New giggle.

- See, me thought they got pretty much silent after the crash, as you would expect. No radio, no transponder signals, no radar signals. Nothing. A long silence. The silence of death... Aargh. Art paused to make sure he got his audience under control.

- But actually, ... Art paused again.

- Another pause and I turn your brain into juice, Fiona said.

50

- Ok, I didn't know you were impatient to learn what I had to say. One of the Rolls Royce engine continued to ping to an Inmarsat satellite for the next six hours after the crash. See? The plane crashed, but one of the reactors continued flying solo. Isn't that amazing?

SEVENTEEN

As Bob was driving up Connecticut avenue towards his comfortable home in Bethesda, he thought about the discussion he'd had with Nicole when he had retired. He had wanted to go to the Sun Belt or someplace cheap next to a lake or the sea. Nicole had vetoed that firmly.

- I don't want you in the house all day. You'll keep on working. You need it. And I need you out.

Maybe she will think differently now that his work meant more than just a good paycheck. A daughter of a French foreign legion colonel, Nicole was plucky in her ways, and not used to complaining. But she hadn't been in the firing line so far. And as General Patton told his man on the eve of D Day, "Every man is scared in his first battle. If he says he's not, he's a liar". He wondered how she would react.

As he opened the door, she looked her normal self, though a bit startled at his dirty beard. He'd forgotten he had slept in his clothes and not even taken time to shave.

- Man you look filthy! Go and have a wash and tell me where you've been!

Which Bob thought was probably what Tony should have said to him. But Tony didn't care anymore. Folks you hired nowadays came with all kind of looks. Some you entertained on purpose to mingle with the bad guys. As you would expect, some looked bad and gradually turned bad. Others were hired looking bad, pretending they were not during the interviews.

As he prepared Nicole her usual frozen margarita, he gave her a sanitized version of both his last couple of days and of her plastic hand grenades. Her immediate reaction was to start looking ahead of the game.

- So if I understand well, you're playing hot and cold. The closer you get to bringing this WikiTi down the harder their punches. I got plastic bombs because you're still off track, but I'll soon know when you start improving your game.

- Well, with the bunch of guys they have downtown, you're pretty safe right now. I won't get any close soon. You should have seen them. They've got the brains of a hedgehog.

- Come on dear. From what you describe they're suffering from positive discrimination.

- You're right, I'm being tough on the hedgehog. There was this guy at the coffee machine. Looked like a turtle. He told me he was an IT freak. So I asked him if he was a kind of geek, could code in all kinds of languages, etc... He said no, not quite, by geek he just meant he had over a thousand friends on Facebook, and spent most of his nights playing games with folks around the world. What is this supposed to mean? The guy wasn't even joking. The police staff their anti-terrorist IT department with Facebook fans. That's probably worse than hiring fans of the New Orleans Pelicans for all I know. At least you've got tactics in basketball. Nicole, what a strange world we live in.

- I don't think the tax payer is rich enough to afford the services of NBA players. Why don't you get this Louis to help you? Maybe Tony can talk him into that?

As they sat in front of the TV together, the headlines news broke out. A Lufthansa Airbus flying Barcelona to Germany had crashed in the Alps. No hope of finding any survivors, no reason for the plane to go down either.

- I'd better get a few hours' sleep, Bob said, tomorrow's going to be a long day.

- Well, every plane that goes down is not a terrorist attack. Nicole said. Especially in the Alps. Remember my grandfather's plane got struck by lightning fifty years ago.
- You're right, but in my line of work, we let others hope for the best, while we plan for the worst.

EIGHTEEN

Then the ashes will return to the earth as it was, and the spirit will return to God who gave it. Vanities of vanities said the preacher, all is vanities.
(Book of Ecclesiastes 12:7)

- Everything needs rules, Louis.
- If you didn't believe in democracy, you had to say so earlier. No use awaking after 2000 years of pretending this was the panacea to human disorder. If you refuse it now, you're like this poker player that keeps bluffing, yet when the time comes to show his hands, he freaks out and says "I fold". Except in the game of life you can't fold. You've got billions of folks out there, who want democracy because they've been told it was good for them, and who finally have found a way to have it. You can't take it away from them, Bob, it's theirs.

Tony had given Bob a green light to go and hire Louis, but that wasn't going to be easy.

- Ok, Louis, democracy, fine, but sending innocent victims to their death isn't democracy, is it?
- Have you ever seen an eel catch its prey? The eel sends an electric wave that takes control of the prey. The eel doesn't even

55

need to touch the fish. Yet you see the fish loses control of its own muscles, turns around and heads straight for the eel. Straight towards death. This is ok? Or you want to stop that too? The fish is innocent. Bob, look around you. It's life. We'll all return to ashes.

- But... if you can prevent it, Louis? If your girl-friend was on that plane, would you do something to lower her score in WikiTi? Would you do something to save her?

- I know what you're getting at, Bob. I'm a man, like you are. Not everyone is ready to sacrifice Isaac. But those deaths are not worth more than the children who are dying in Africa. I know, nobody cares for them up in DC. Face it, you're just part of system, Bob. Another brick in the wall. Bottom line, you're financed by the insurance companies. And they're goddam freaking out. Wetting their pants. And that's right. They'll go bankrupt if they lose a couple of airplanes. Lobbyists are sleeping at the White house these days. Google alone had hundreds of meetings just this year with White house officials...

- Louis, I need you. Those victims need you. Wiki... Action needs you. You can't let your tool become a tool of death. This is not what you wanted. You wanted rice to flow to Ethiopia. Remember. Not children to be thrown into the Alps.

- That's not WikiTi. Not all planes that crash are WikiTi's.

- Ok, wrong one. I still need you.

- The system is no longer mine, Bob. It's open source. If the world wants to take control of the US sewage system, and pollute all our drinking water, it can. This is like nuclear deterrent. It's a cold war. Isn't it better than all other wars?

- You can make it evolve before it's too late. Come with me to DC, and I'll show you the kind of folks we don't want to see getting access to your tool. It's not bright and rosy.

- I'm not coming with you, but here's what I'm going to do. I'm going to try and set up some parameters in there. I can't promise anything.

As Bob got up to leave, Louis shook his hand and said.

- By the way, I wanted to tell you, your score is going up pretty fast in WikiTi. You'd better watch out.

NINETEEN

Bob had decided he needed some team building with the team, so he'd invited Fiona and her three direct reports to one of DC's best burger houses. Two of them were still sulking so he'd only got Fiona and Tamid. But he wasn't too fussed about it. He'd work his way up from there. If he could turn those two in his favor the others would likely follow.

- To be honest, Fiona said, biting into her giant burger and throwing juice on all three of them without seeming to notice or to bother at all, we knew those guys were out there. We'd kept telling Tony.

Nobody is surprised these days, Bob thought. Trick is to tell that you already knew with a poker face. It's a question of practice. And those that got up the ladder had their share.

- So why not work on it, tell the White House.
- Well, first of all, because they're not interested.
- What do you mean?
- That's why they give this type of work to a consultant. The rest of us are busy doing serious stuff.
- Makes sense, Bob answered. His usual two-way answer.
- Since 9/11, politicians need simple stories. And the only story the press can handle right now is Al Qaeda. So each time some crazy guy has broken into our systems, diverted a plane, or blew himself apart, we've had to make up an Al Qaeda story. Al Qaeda Indonesia, Al Qaeda Maghreb, or whatever place did it. We've now got quite a collection of Al Qaeda's. Ok, we've got the

57

best communication agencies helping us, we wouldn't be that creative alone. This is the police, not Sony studios.
- In the police, half of our job is to make up stories. In PowerPoint mostly, Tamid interjected in support of her boss.
Fiona continued.
- It's like an HBO series. We have to come up regularly with a story. We have seasons of our own. We're competing for air time and audience with The Wire, or Game of Thrones. And they're pretty good. If the public gets tired of Kima, she gets a bullet and she's out of the series. Same with Ben Laden. A good video, pictures of the president in his action room looking concerned and out goes bad guy number one. "Panem and Circenses", she concluded thinking Latin culture may impress the retired police guy in plain clothes.
- Is this why you joined? Bob asked trying to get them back to more meaty stuff.
- You join for the pay check, and short of prostitution you do more or less everything you're asked to do.

Bob focused from then onwards on his initial goal of team building, made them laugh, and told them old jokes. Fiona and Tamid added theirs, so his goal was probably met.

- You guys walk back to the office. I need to buy a birthday present for my gal. I'll see you there, said Fiona as they parted on the curb.
- We've got strong personalities in the service, Tamid said as they walked slowly back down the block. But they aren't bad. It's just that we keep making the same mistakes over and over again. As a team we're not focused.
- How good are they at doing IT stuff, Tamid?
- Well, you know the key issue for us here is recruiting. Seventy five percent of IT graduates in a class at John Hopkins are not US citizens so we can't hire them. So that's five to ten left for us to recruit from. We pay them less, our careers are less attractive, and Snowden has discouraged the others. So we recruit folks that don't

even have IT degrees often times. We just have to train them ourselves. And we work our way up from there. It's tough but we have to make it work. I'm a PhD chemist, but as a manager that's ok.

- So not really the cyber warriors you'd think the first world power would have.

Tamid chuckled, and went on.

- You know, I like the way you work. I understand what you mean, and I think we'll get some good work done. The group needs some vision. It's got authority. But it lacks vision. I just want you to know I'm with you. The others are not against you, they're just not with you right now. You may need to make some people changes if you want the whole group behind. I think Tony would support that.

- Well, thanks Tamid. I'm going to need all the help I can get. We're up against the Big One. And we didn't see it coming. We may not have time for a team change. I get the feeling it's going to heat up real fast. It's hurricane season right now. And the power is about to be unleashed.

TWENTY

With all your heart, honor your father, and never forget what your mother suffered.
(Book of Sirach 7:27)

Nicole was walking with her son Jeff, back from his karate lesson. It always made bystanders smile to watch this elegant lady in high heels walk with an enthusiastic teenager in kimono and flip flops. Jeff was getting ready for his blue belt test on Saturday, and was jumping up and down as they walked, showing his mum all the kicks and punches he had to do to pass. She was proud of her young stag, though wished he cleared the puddles with a greater safety margin. Stains wouldn't go away easily on her tight fitted white leather trousers.

It seemed like it had just stopped raining, with the water still rushing in the gutters. And the pedestrian traffic hadn't yet caught up with the change of weather. Nicole kept as far as she could away from the cars, most of which didn't bother to slow down, splashing their way by them.

She heard the car coming, slowing down for once. In the corner of her eyes she saw the door open, and hands grab Jeff lifting him up in air and literally sweeping him off into the car. Trained as a tennis athlete to leap in all directions to prevent the ball from hitting the ground, Nicole dived towards the car and the disappearing kid, catching his ankle as she hit the ground. The car was gathering speed, but she held on, her long body gradually moving under the car. Still, she wouldn't let go.

She heard the bone crack as the car rolled over her leg. She got dragged to the next crossroad, where a passer-by grabbed Nicole away from the beneath the car, forcing her to let go, and saving her from sure death.

TWENTY-ONE

- I told you your score was getting high quickly, Louis said. Maybe he was on loud speaker, because his voice was coming from far.
- Sure. Did you expect me to quit?
- So I've got a few options for you. Do you want me to list them out? By the sound of his voice, Louis was probably upside down, hanging with his toe nail from his climbing wall over his computer. Bob felt like the guy talking to spider man in the movie.
- I only see one, you get into WikiTi and lower my son's score to zero.
- Well, it's not that easy you see. It's open source. Not Louis.com. And I don't give a freaking shit about your son to be honest.
- Ok, so what options have we got?

When the Intensive Care unit had called him at the office to say his wife was on the block and his son kidnapped, Bob had missed a heartbeat. It reminded him of when his dad had received a call in February 68 announcing that Bob's elder brother Jim, had gone down in the Tet offensive. He felt a huge pain in his chest. Bob's first call was to Tony. The boss had been pretty calm about it. "Steady now, we'll get him back. You continue on the IT front, and I'm getting DC police to put road blocks up". His second call had been to Louis. Calling Fiona into his office and letting the team know would wait for now.

- First option, Louis continued. I do nothing. Second option, I get your son out, but that burns my administrator credentials and I'm out of WikiTi for good. I'd hate that, and I wouldn't be of much use

62

for the next hit that they'll make at you. Your team in DC is creating a lot of negative noise on the web, right now. They aren't likely to find anything, you know, they're just getting your score up.

- Let's get back to your options. How long is your list?

- Third option, Louis continued unfazed, I plug in that Nicole's in a wheelchair, her tennis career gone for good, and there's a good chance that gives you enough bonus points to release your son.

- Ok go for it. Be quick.

- You need to tell me which option. It's fine to go quick, by I need a direction.

- Third option, ironman.

- Do you want to check with Nicole first? She may not like you deciding on her tennis career without consulting.

- It's a man's world, Louis.

- Ok, go to hell. Let me know when the kid shows up.

Louis just hung up. Beep Beep Beep.

Ok Bob thought, now for my specially gifted team. He pressed his loudspeaker and dialed Fiona's.

- Gather the whole team for me, I've got an announcement to make.

- Look, if you continue to manage this whole team like a summer camp...

Bob cut her short.

- My son's just been kidnapped.

- Holy shit.

Bob heard her shout like a loudspeaker in a Rock festival. "Everyone come out here, we need all your wits. Now!"

She may not have many qualities Bob thought. But she's got a hell of a voice.

TWENTY-TWO

For the next twenty four hours, DC transformed itself in a gigantic manhunt. Most of which you could follow on TV. Journalists had quickly made the link with Nicole, so the hospital had to be cordoned off too. Bob insisted that Bob junior still went to school. Doing otherwise felt like surrendering. So the school ended up with as many policemen around it, than it had kids inside. Helicopters and the latest acquisition of semi-planes semi-helicopters kept filling the sky with the noise of their propellers. You couldn't go to a mall, you couldn't go on the streets. DC was under siege. The police was out. One of theirs had been hit.

Bob wasn't sure though, that Jeff wasn't already far off. Maybe he'd been rushed to the sea, put on a container ship out there, and was on his way to Asia or some Latin American country. And there'd be no return. Ever. If Louis was right, you couldn't beat WikiTi. Not even the entire police force of this country. You couldn't beat the entire population of the world, with most of them helping with infinitely small actions to make Jeff disappear from the radar.

On the second front, Nicole's operation was turning out more complex than the surgeons had initially thought. She was still asleep and had returned to the block for more operations. Her days were no longer in danger although her main leg artery had been badly damaged. Had Bob had an opportunity to talk to her quickly after the incident he would have managed the stress easily. But this dragging on was slowly taking his nerves down. Not being the

64

extravert type, he didn't really have any close relative or friend to confide into. And going fly fishing, horse riding or to the gym, which he did when under stress didn't look right. He could imagine the headlines in the morning papers "Chief detective goes for leisurely ride in the park while spouse fights for life". In the past he'd had a small team around him to keep his nose in the operations. But you couldn't call Fiona's team comfort. Some had started crying when they heard Jeff was kidnapped and Nicole injured. He'd told them to continue working hard, but he could feel that the news had taken its toll, and they would spend the rest of the day talking in twos or three, whispering whenever he would approach. He guessed the only thing they would eventually do on their computers was read the news bulletins to have more to share among themselves. Some just avoided his gaze, others made unfortunate remarks. Art giggled at him and said "no news good news". Fiona alone kept her head and continued hating him, blurting out in his office.

- I knew this would happen. You're managing this case like a walk on the beach.

Bob didn't have the energy to ask her to get out, so she kept on.

- You should leave this damn department to me. Get out of here and go to your wife. You're retired! You're too old to stand this.

- Yes, Bob thought, especially you.

Eventually he left the office, picked his younger son from school, which he never did, and both went to the hospital. As Nicole was still out, they ate at the hospital's restaurant a quick meal that made them wish they had chosen another place.

They went back to Nicole, who opened her eyes once but immediately went back to sleep. When Bob junior almost fell off his chair from exhaustion, Bob lifted him up, and slowly walked out of the hospital and then drove home. He had been wondering how Nicole would take it, but had never thought he would take it so badly.

TWENTY-THREE

Jeff re-appeared as mysteriously as he had disappeared, a couple of days later. The same day Nicole got out of the hospital. First thing Bob did was call Louis.

- Louis, Jeff is back, thanks.
- You're welcome.
- Look, he's got a tattoo, "Redeemed" written in gothic letters on his left shoulder.
- Yeah. I hope you don't mind. That's the little concession I had to make to get him free. Sequestered folks in WikiTi are never supposed to resurface. Like the MAS passengers. They don't necessarily die. But they don't resurface. Your son's an exception.
- Great.
- You know it's this reincarnation stuff that comes from having all those geeks from India influencing the design of WikiTi. They believe in reincarnation. And it's ok, I guess. If Texans were coding instead of cracking shale right now, WikiTi would probably shoot people. So yeah, you're lucky this time.
- Still, this tattoo, you could have chosen some smaller fonts.
- We'll remember that, Bob, when your time comes. But look at how big the Abercrombie logo sticks out your son's hoody, and you may think differently. Maybe he likes it like it is.
- Abercrombie is a brand.
- So is WikiTi. And my bet it soon will become the world's number one.
- Ok, take care.

- Oh, by the way, you remember that plane that crashed in the Alps?

- That was WikiTi after all?

- No, but we've got a patch.

- A what? A lead?

- Next time a pilot goes suicidal, if WikiTi votes against the crash, the pilot will automatically lose control.

- Really?

- Yeah, isn't it cool?

- So what happens, you take control and then what?

- It doesn't have to last long. As soon as the pilot sees he's lost control, we'd expect his suicidal freak to vanish. He can still cut his veins in the restrooms. But we'll steady the plane. We could also lower the oxygen in the cabin to give him a bit of a scare actually. That's an idea.

- How's my score?

- Relatively steady now. You're on watch.

- Let me know if anything changes.

- You'll find out buddy.

THE END

Shut up the words, and seal the book, to the time of the End: many shall run to and fro, and knowledge shall be increased.
(Book of Daniel 12:4)